THE ROCKET

MIKE LEONETTI

ILLUSTRATIONS BY
GREG BANNING

SCHOLASTIC CANADA LTD.
Toronto New York London Auckland Sydney
Mexico City New Delhi Hong Kong Buenos Aires

ACKNOWLEDGEMENTS

The books of the following authors were used to research this story: Mike Bynum, Roch Carrier, Charles Coleman, Stan Fishler, Ed Fitkin, Trent Frayne, Chrys Goyens, Doug Hunter, Dick Irvin, Brian Kendall, Ron McAllister, Chris McDonell, Brian McFarlane, Andy O'Brien, Frank Orr, Sheldon Posen, Maurice Richard, Celine Steinmetz. Magazines reviewed: *Hockey Pictorial, Hockey Illustrated, Hockey Digest, Sports Illustrated.* Newspapers consulted: *Hockey Now, Globe and Mail, Montreal Daily Herald, The Gazette, Toronto Star, Vaughan Citizen.* Reference Books and Guides used: *Total NHL, NHL Stanley Cup Playoffs Fact Guide, Montreal Canadiens Media Guide.* Web site consulted: www.canadiens.nhl.com. Movie: *The Rocket.*

While the events described and some of the characters in this book may be based on actual historical events and real people, Andre is a fictional character, created by the author, and his story is a work of fiction.

Scholastic Canada Ltd.
604 King Street West, Toronto, Ontario M5V 1E1, Canada

Scholastic Inc.
557 Broadway, New York, NY 10012, USA

Scholastic Australia Pty Limited
PO Box 579, Gosford, NSW 2250, Australia

Scholastic New Zealand Limited
Private Bag 94407, Greenmount, Auckland, New Zealand

Scholastic Children's Books
Euston House, 24 Eversholt Street, London NW1 1DB, UK

Photograph on page 30 © HHOF Images.

Library and Archives Canada Cataloguing in Publication

Leonetti, Mike, 1958-
The Rocket / Mike Leonetti ; illustrations by Greg Banning.
ISBN 978-0-545-98966-4
1. Richard, Maurice, 1921-2000—Juvenile fiction.
I. Banning, Greg II. Title.
PS8573.E58734R63 2009a   jC813'.54   C2009-903230-9

ISBN-10 0-545-98966-3

6 5 4 3 2 1   Printed in Singapore   09 10 11 12 13

"Andre! Are you ready to go? It's almost time for your game."

"Almost ready, Dad," I said as I pulled on my sweater.

My school hockey team, St. Marguerite, was playing St. Francois. As much as I loved playing hockey, I almost didn't want to go.

I knew as soon as I hit the ice I'd start hearing how I'd never be as good as my older brother Marcel. Everyone said he'd play in the National Hockey League one day, maybe for the Montreal Canadiens. He was a defenseman and had won lots of awards. He'd even led his teams to championships. Sometimes I thought about switching to another sport just so I wouldn't have to hear how I'd never be as good as him.

"Come on, Andre . . . smile," Dad said as we got in the car. "It's just a game."

We took to the ice on our outdoor rink. As soon as I got the puck,
I heard someone say, "He's not as good as his brother." Once,
I fanned on a pass and heard, "Aw, come on! Your brother wouldn't
have missed that!"

Then I heard some people call out to a smaller player on the other
team. "Hey, where's your big brother? Is he going to fight for
you?" He was getting it just as bad as I was.

I didn't know him, but he was great. He could stickhandle and shoot the puck, and he scored both goals for their team. It seemed like he had the puck the whole time he was on the ice.

I could still hear people comparing me to my brother, but I tried to stay focused. I even scored a goal in our 3–2 win.

When I got home, Marcel asked me how the game went.

"We won," I said. "And I scored a goal."

"That's great!"

"But of course I had to listen to people say that I'll never be as good as you," I said.

Marcel could tell I was upset. "Don't worry about making mistakes, and don't listen to them. Just play your game and you'll be fine."

I knew Marcel was trying to make me feel better, but I didn't feel like listening to him. I wondered if I could ever escape his shadow.

Marcel and I both loved the Montreal Canadiens. They hadn't been very good the past few years, even though they had made the playoffs last season. But the 1943–44 season was supposed to be a good one. They had a new goalie, Bill Durnan, along with other great players like Toe Blake, Elmer Lach, Ray Getliffe and Phil Watson. Our family would listen to the game on the radio every Saturday night and celebrate every Montreal goal. We hoped the team would have a chance to play for the Stanley Cup.

There was one player who could really score — Maurice Richard. He was only 22 years old and from Montreal. Even though he'd been injured a lot, this season he'd come ready to play. He would take off so fast once he got the puck on his stick, a teammate called him a rocket. The nickname stuck, and soon people were calling him "The Rocket."

Coach Dick Irvin put Richard on a line with Blake and Lach, which people called "The Punch Line." Richard scored 32 goals and had 22 assists, and the three of them led the Canadiens to first place, winning 38 of 50 games.

Following how well the Canadiens were doing took our minds off the war that was going on in Europe. It really helped to keep our spirits up.

My father worked at a plant where they made supplies for the war. One night he came home and told us they had someone new at the factory — Maurice Richard! He worked at the plant most days but still played for the Canadiens at night. Dad said Richard was pretty modest and didn't talk about hockey too much. Dad did ask him about the three hat tricks he had already scored. The Rocket said you need a little luck to do that. He also said that he could help us get tickets to the playoffs!

My school team also had a good year, although St. Francois beat us in the playoffs. I scored ten goals in the season, which was pretty good, but that kid from St. Francois was the top player in our league. I'd see him when a bunch of us played out on the Back River. He owned the puck. It seemed like it never left his stick. He was pretty quiet, but he would still get taunted by some of the older boys about his brother. It didn't seem to bother him much, though. He just kept playing his best.

By late March it was time for the playoffs, and I was excited about the Canadiens' chances of winning the Stanley Cup. They faced the Toronto Maple Leafs in the first round. Dad took Marcel to the first game at the Forum, but the Canadiens lost 3–1 — their first loss at home all year long.

When they got home, Dad said, "Andre, you're coming to the next game. Maybe they'll have better luck with you there." My first NHL game!

As we walked into the Forum you could feel the excitement in the air. Everyone knew the Canadiens had to win this game. After we took our seats, I noticed a familiar face — the boy from St. Francois. We said hello to each other as he and his father took their seats next to us.

Neither team could score in the first period. The crowd was on edge. Each time Richard got the puck, people seemed to hold their breath, waiting for something to happen. From our seats, you could see the Rocket's black hair, and eyes that seemed to be on fire. His number 9 blazed up and down the ice.

"That Richard is pretty good, eh?" I said to the kid next to me. "He plays on the wing like me, so he's my favourite player."

"Yeah, he's very good. And he really likes to score," he said.

We waited for the second period to start and talked a little more.

"Don't you hate it when they compare you to your brother?" I asked. "People always compare me to my brother, too."

"Yeah, it bothers me," he said. "I just remind them of my name, so they know we're different people. But they still tell me that I'll never be as good as him."

"Me too," I said. I looked around. "Why are people looking and pointing at you and your father? Do they know your brother?"

He smiled. "Uhm . . . yes."

"Geez, that's tough," I said.

In the second period, the Rocket was still having trouble getting away from the checker the Maple Leafs had put on him. But then Montreal defenseman Mike McMahon passed the puck to Lach who passed it to Richard. He gave the Leafs goalie a fake before shooting it in. 1–0 for Montreal!

"Canadiens goal by MAAUUREEECE REEECHAARD!" the announcer called. The Forum erupted in cheers. The boy's father pumped his fist and yelled, "Maurice!"

A few seconds later, Blake and Lach set up Richard for another goal — it was 2–0! The crowd got a little nervous when Toronto scored a goal with Richard in the penalty box. But then, just before the period ended, The Rocket drilled in a shot from about 20 feet out for his third goal of the period. A hat trick!

"Wow! The Rocket is really going tonight," I said to the boy. "Can you imagine if he were your brother? That'd be a lot of pressure."

"Yeah," he said, smiling. "I can."

In the third period The Rocket got his fourth goal of the game when he hit a rolling puck into the Toronto net to make it 4–1. Then he swept a rebound into the net as he fell to the ice. Five goals in one game! The Forum went crazy! The fans gave Richard a standing ovation.

Montreal won the game 5–1 — all five goals scored by Richard! Everyone waited for the three stars of the game to be called. The announcer came on and named Maurice Richard as the third star. Only the third? With five goals? But then the announcer named him as the second star — and finally, the first! The crowd cheered wildly. The Rocket came out each time, and the crowd saluted him.

The boy from St. Francois was cheering louder than anyone. He turned to me and said, "Nobody can score like my brother!"

"What?" I said. "Your brother?"

"Yes. Maurice is my brother. My name is Henri Richard." He smiled at me. "Someday I hope to play with him for the Canadiens, and we can win the Stanley Cup together." Henri smiled and looked back to the ice where The Rocket was skating off. You could tell he was really proud.

The next day my mom took me to an ice carnival where Richard was signing autographs. I brought my stick to be signed.

When it was my turn I said, "That was a great game you played last night, Mr. Richard."

"*Merci*," he said quietly.

Coach Irvin was sitting beside him. "That was the greatest one-man performance you will ever see in a playoff game," he said to me.

"Yes, sir," I said. I turned to The Rocket. "I sat next to your brother Henri at the game."

"Really? Henri's played hockey for a couple of years now," he said. "He's usually the best player on the ice."

"I play against him in the school league. He's really good," I said.

As we turned to leave, I thought how nice it was that the Richards were proud of each other. It got me thinking about me and Marcel. I was proud of him, too.

The Canadiens beat the Maple Leafs in that first round and then played the Chicago Black Hawks for the Cup. On the night of the final game, our family sat around the radio to listen. We cheered as The Rocket scored twice, and went wild when Blake scored the winning goal in overtime. Marcel and I jumped up and hugged each other. The Canadiens had won their first Stanley Cup in 14 years!

Seeing how Maurice and Henri Richard were so proud of each other made me see Marcel differently. Maybe one day we could play hockey on the same team, too.

The next season he and I started going to each other's games. I also saw how helpful his advice could be. It didn't matter anymore to me what anybody said; if I wasn't as good as Marcel, that was alright.

Meeting the Richards made me really appreciate Marcel. I was proud to have him as my brother.

ABOUT MAURICE "ROCKET" RICHARD

Maurice Richard was born on August 4, 1921, in Montreal, Quebec. He first joined the Montreal Canadiens for the 1942–43 season but only played in 16 games before he was injured. In 1943–44 he registered 54 points in 46 games and then added another 12 goals in the playoffs as the Canadiens won the Stanley Cup. In 1944–45 Richard became the first player in NHL history to score 50 goals in one season, a mark still considered the sign of a great season. He was also the first to score 500 career goals and was an eight-time winner of the Stanley Cup. Richard became team captain in 1956 and was named to the NHL's First All-Star Team eight times. During his career Richard notched 83 game-winning goals and finished with 544 goals and 944 points in 978 games. He also recorded 82 playoff goals (including six overtime winners), for a total of 133 points in 126 post-season games. Richard was elected to the Hockey Hall of Fame in 1961. In 1999 the NHL decided to recognize the leading goal scorer of each season with the Maurice "Rocket" Richard Trophy. Richard died in 2000 at the age of 78; his funeral was broadcast on television across Canada. He is still recognized as the greatest player in the history of the Montreal Canadiens.

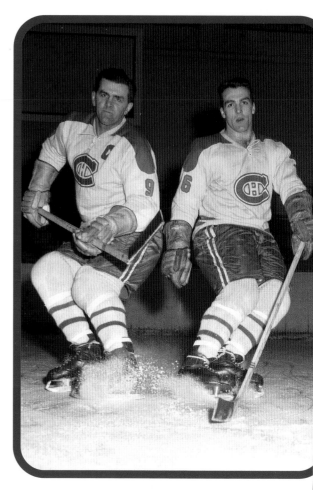

ABOUT HENRI RICHARD

Henri Richard was born on February 29, 1936, in Montreal and joined the Canadiens for the 1955–56 season. He scored 358 career goals and had 688 assists in 1,256 games between 1955–56 and 1974–1975. Henri was considered small at 5'7", but he had a big heart and a strong desire to succeed. By the time his career was over, he had won a remarkable 11 Stanley Cups — five of which he shared with his brother Maurice (1955–1956 to 1959–1960), reaching his dream of sharing championships with his older sibling. Known as the "Pocket Rocket," Richard scored two Stanley Cup-winning goals (in 1966 and 1971) and was a league all-star four times. He was Montreal's captain between 1971 and 1975 and was named winner of the Masterton Trophy in 1974. Henri Richard was elected to the Hockey Hall of Fame in 1979.